Dear Parent:
Your child's love of reading starts here!

Every child learns to read in a different way and at his or her own speed. Some go back and forth between reading levels and read favorite books again and again. Others read through each level in order. You can help your young reader improve and become more confident by encouraging his or her own interests and abilities. From books your child reads with you to the first books he or she reads alone, there are I Can Read Books for every stage of reading:

SHARED READING
Basic language, word repetition, and whimsical illustrations, ideal for sharing with your emergent reader

BEGINNING READING
Short sentences, familiar words, and simple concepts for children eager to read on their own

READING WITH HELP
Engaging stories, longer sentences, and language play for developing readers

READING ALONE
Complex plots, challenging vocabulary, and high-interest topics for the independent reader

ADVANCED READING
Short paragraphs, chapters, and exciting themes for the perfect bridge to chapter books

I Can Read Books have introduced children to the joy of reading since 1957. Featuring award-winning authors and illustrators and a fabulous cast of beloved characters, I Can Read Books set the standard for beginning readers.

A lifetime of discovery begins with the magical words **"I Can Read!"**

Visit www.icanread.com for information
on enriching your child's reading experience.

I Can Read!™

SHARED
My First
READING

GOING TO THE FIREHOUSE

BY MERCER MAYER

HarperCollins*Publishers*

*To Arden and Benjamin,
our two new high school graduates!*

HarperCollins®, 🔖®, and I Can Read Book® are trademarks of HarperCollins Publishers.

Library of Congress catalog card number: 2007929409
ISBN 978-0-06-083546-0 (trade bdg.) — ISBN 978-0-06-083545-3 (pbk.)
16 SCP 10 9 8 7   ❖   First Edition

Today my class is going
to the firehouse!
I dress like a fireman.
Time to fight a fire!

This is Fireman Joe.

This is his dog, Sparky.

Sparky is a fire dog.

Fireman Joe has boots.

He has a jacket.

He has a helmet.

I have boots.

I have a jacket.

I do not have a helmet.

Joe slides down the pole.
Sparky howls.
That is what he does
when there is a fire.

We see a fire truck.

It is big.

It is red.

It has hoses and a ladder.

Joe checks the hoses.

He lets me help.

Whoosh goes the water.

This hose is working fine.

Joe checks the ladder.

He goes up and up.

He is in the sky.

Hello, Fireman Joe!

Joe checks the siren.

It goes Ooo! Eee! Ooo!

The siren is very loud.

I cover my ears.

Joe tells us about fires.

He tells us smoke goes up.

When smoke goes up,

we must go down to the floor.

I get on the floor.

Joe tells us what to do if we
are on fire.

Stop,

drop,

and roll!

I stop, drop, and roll!

Fireman Joe smiles.

He has a surprise.

He reaches into his truck.

Helmets for everyone!

I put on my helmet.

Joe tells me I will be
a good fireman one day.

Ding! Ding! goes the fire alarm.

I wave good-bye to Fireman Joe.

I wave good-bye to Sparky.

Time to fight a fire!

Fireman Joe is ready to go!
Sparky is, too.